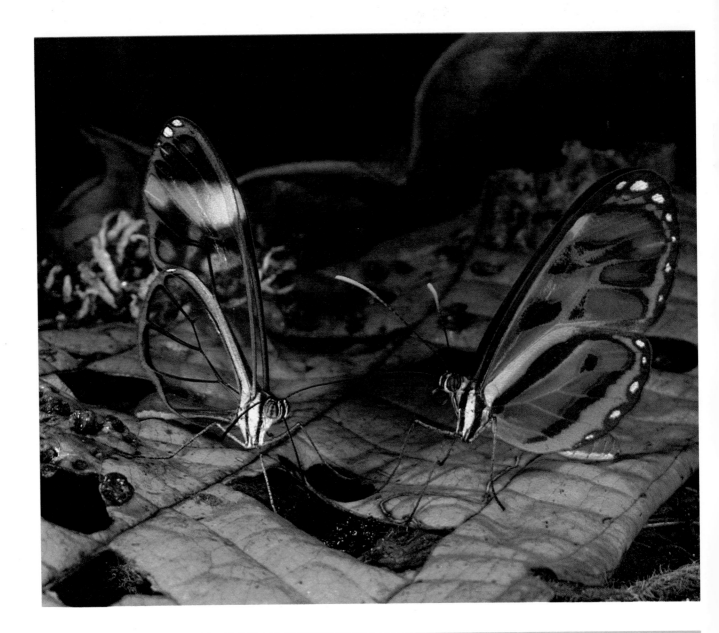

Discovering
BUTTERFLIES AND MOTHS

Keith Porter

Illustrations by Wendy Meadway

The Bookwright Press
New York

All photographs from Oxford Scientific Films

First Paperback Edition 1990
ISBN 0-531-18364-5

First published in the
United States in 1986 by
The Bookwright Press
387 Park Avenue South
New York, NY 10016

First published in 1986 by
Wayland (Publishers) Limited
61 Western Road, Hove
East Sussex, BN3 1JD, England

© Copyright 1986 Wayland (Publishers) Limited

Library of Congress Catalog Card Number: 85-73664

Typeset by Alphabet Limited
Printed in Italy by G. Canale & C. S.p.A., Turin

Cover *African monarch butterflies gather together at night to sleep.*

Frontispiece *Clearwing butterflies feeding on the forest floor.*

Contents

1 Introducing Butterflies and Moths

A small tortoiseshell butterfly on a buddleia flower.

Butterflies and Moths as Insects

Butterflies and moths are very beautiful creatures. They belong to the group of animals we call insects. Insects are the most common animals in the world and they include wasps, bees, beetles, and flies. Three out of every four animals are insects.

Insects are made up of three main body parts. The head is at the front end of the body. The middle part is called the **thorax**, and this is where the legs and wings are fixed. The last, and largest, part is called the **abdomen.** This is often divided into segments, rather like a worm's body.

The head, thorax, and abdomen do different jobs and all are made from a hard material called chitin (pronounced kite-in). This gives the insect its shape. Unlike most larger animals, insects do not have bones. Instead, the chitin forms a shell that is a kind of skin, skeleton, and suit of armor, all rolled into one.

Insects are divided into about thirty groups. Butterflies and moths make up one group called the *Lepidoptera*. This name means "scale-winged" and tells us that the wings are covered with tiny flat scales. The scales are actually special flattened hairs. They overlap and lie on the wing like tiles on a roof. Each scale is colored, and this helps to produce the beautiful patterns found on the wings of butterflies and moths.

On its head you can clearly see this moth's feelers, which it uses to taste and smell.

The Bodies of Butterflies and Moths

Butterflies and moths have two large eyes that cover most of the head. These are called **compound eyes**. Each compound eye is made up from thousands of tiny **lenses**. Each lens sees only a small part of the whole "picture." Butterflies and moths can see colors, and they are able to detect movement and shapes.

Every butterfly and moth has a pair of feelers, or **antennae**, on its head. These are used to "taste" the air and plants, and act rather like our tongue and nose together. Butterfly antennae are always thin with a thick knob at the tip. Moths have differently shaped antennae from butterflies. Some moths have long, hair-like antennae; others have branched, feather-like ones.

Most butterflies and moths feed on

A close-up of an oak silk moth's head showing its feathery antennae.

the sugary liquid called **nectar**, which is found in flowers. They suck this up through a long, thin "tongue," or **proboscis**. When not in use, this tubelike proboscis is coiled up like a spring, under the head.

The thorax is the "engine" part of any insect's body. It is packed with strong muscles, which move the legs and wings. Like most insects,

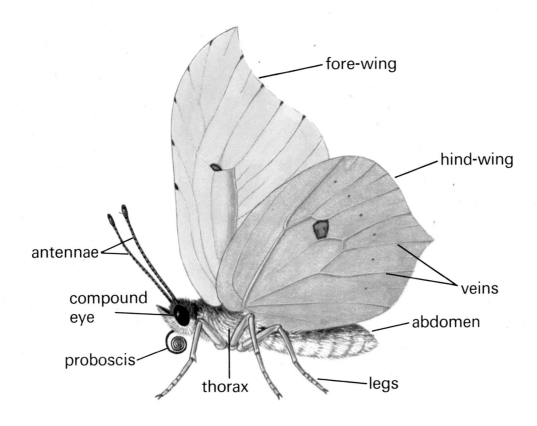

fore-wing

hind-wing

antennae

veins

compound eye

abdomen

proboscis

thorax

legs

butterflies and moths have two pairs of wings and three pairs of legs. Each wing is like a thin sandwich. The "bread" is a very thin sheet of chitin, while the "filling" contains air spaces and tiny tubes called **veins**. A type of blood flows through the veins.

This is a brimstone butterfly.

The abdomen is the softest part of the body of a butterfly or moth. It contains the stomach and is the place where eggs are made and kept until they are ready to be laid.

The owlet moth is the world's largest.

Different Shapes and Sizes

There are over 160,000 types of butterflies and moths in the world. Most of this huge number are moths; only 20,000 types of butterflies are known. Most butterflies and moths live in hot countries, especially in tropical forests.

The largest moth is a type of owlet moth from Brazil which is 30 cm (1 ft) from wing tip to wing tip. The smallest are tiny moths only 2 mm (.08 in) across. The largest butterfly is a birdwing, which can be 28 cm (11 in) across the wing tips. One of the smallest butterflies is the dwarf blue from South Africa. It has a wing span of 14 mm (½ in).

It is often difficult to tell the difference between a butterfly and a moth. One of the best ways is to look at their antennae. There may be other differences too. We can say that most butterflies are brightly colored and fly in the day. They also hold their wings together and upright when at rest. Most moths are dull colored and fly at night. Their bodies are often fatter and more furry than a butterfly's. Moths usually rest with their wings held flat, sticking out from their bodies.

Butterflies and moths come in every color under the sun. Some are bright yellow, red, and green; others are

The moon moth has long wing tails.

shiny blue, just like polished metal. A few butterflies and moths have clear wings with hardly any scales and therefore very little pattern.

Many butterflies and moths have strangely shaped wings. Their wings may have jagged edges or "tails," like those of the swallowtail butterflies. Some silk moths have clear "windows" in their wings. A few types of moths have very tiny wings that are of no use for flying.

2
The Life Cycle of Butterflies and Moths

A milkweed butterfly larva hatches from the egg.

From Egg to Adult

All butterflies and moths go through four stages before they are fully grown. Each begins life as a tiny egg, out of which hatches a small caterpillar or **larva**. During its life the caterpillar changes its skin several times, each time becoming bigger.

Caterpillars grow in stages because of the way their bodies are made. Their skin is tough and does not expand as they grow, so the caterpillar has to burst out of its old skin and form a new, larger skin, in order to grow.

After four or five changes of skin, the caterpillar stops feeding and turns into a **pupa**. The pupa does not feed and usually stays quite still. It is covered with a hard case, inside which the adult butterfly or moth slowly takes shape.

After a period of weeks or months,

the butterfly or moth emerges from the pupa by splitting open the hard case. The newly emerged adult looks very bedraggled. Its wings are tiny and crumpled; they have to be pumped up to size by forcing blood through the veins. Within an hour or so, the butterfly or moth begins to look more like a real adult. The wings are held straight out, to dry and harden, ready for the first flight.

Adult butterflies and moths never grow any bigger. Unlike the caterpillars, they cannot change their skin. They fly off to feed, find a mate, and lay their eggs, to begin the cycle all over again. Most butterflies and moths take a whole year to pass from egg to adult. Some, however, take only a few weeks, while others may need several years.

A newly-emerged Gulf fritillary butterfly clings to its empty pupal case.

Life as an Egg

The eggs of butterflies and moths come in many shapes. All are tiny, the largest being only 3 mm (⅛ in) across.

The simplest eggs look like tiny pearls. Others look very strange and spikey.

A Gulf fritillary butterfly egg.

The shell of butterfly and moth eggs is made from chitin, like the outside skin of all insects. This tough shell protects the contents and prevents them from drying out.

The eggshell is not usually smooth, but is shaped into bumps, knobs, or ridges. These make the eggs look strange and beautiful if seen through a microscope. The bumps help to make the shell strong. They act like the girders on buildings and bridges.

Some eggs have transparent shells and the tiny developing caterpillar can often be seen through the walls. Other eggs have colored shells that help to hide them from enemies.

Inside the egg is a tiny watery world in which the caterpillar takes shape. Each egg contains yolk, just as in a chicken's egg. This is used as food by the tiny caterpillar as it grows.

Some types of butterflies or moths have eggs that do not hatch for

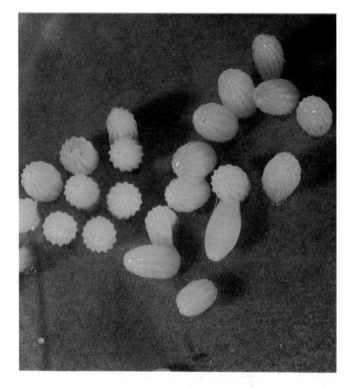

Cabbage white butterfly eggs on a cabbage leaf.

almost nine months. These eggs have to protect the caterpillars over long, cold winters, or through hot, dry summers. Other eggs hatch after only a few days.

Life as a Caterpillar

Caterpillars are usually long, worm-like creatures. Their soft bodies are divided into thirteen or fourteen segments and at the front there is a hard, round head.

Caterpillars are very different from their parents. They have eight pairs of legs, twelve tiny eyes, and biting jaws. They can also spin their own silk.

The front three pairs of legs are called true legs. They are made of hard tubes of chitin and can bend. Each has a sharp claw at the end. The

You can see this silk moth caterpillar's jaws and several tiny eyes.

A caterpillar's prolegs showing the ring of hooks at the end of each one.

other five pairs are fixed to the middle and back segments of the body. They are called false legs, or **prolegs**. Each proleg is a soft stump with a ring of hooks around the bottom. These hooks are useful for clinging to slippery leaves.

The caterpillar's eyes are called **simple eyes**. They cannot be used to see a complete picture of their surroundings, but they can usually see colors and they help the caterpillar to tell night from day.

The caterpillar's first job is to bite its way out of the egg. Most types then make their first meal out of the old eggshell, which is very nourishing. The caterpillar then starts to feed on other things – usually plants of some kind. Caterpillars spend all their lives eating. The food they eat is stored as fat and later used to build the body of the adult butterfly or moth.

Most caterpillars take a month or two to grow to full size. Some take several months to complete their growth. They may have a resting stage over the winter or through a hot dry summer. A few types of caterpillars can grow to full size in only a week or so.

Strange Foods for Caterpillars

A moth caterpillar eating a sawfly larva.

Most caterpillars eat the leaves or stems of plants. Indeed, every plant in the world has at least one type of caterpillar that feeds on it. Other caterpillars eat wood, roots, or even other insects. The goat moth caterpillar spends three or four years eating wood inside an apple tree.

Among the strangest types of moths are those whose caterpillars eat feathers, fur or wool. They are usually found in old birds' nests, or among the remains of dead animals. Today, many of these moths are common pests in houses.

The clothes moth is found all over the world. The adult is a small brown moth, which may drink water but cannot eat clothes. The clothes moth caterpillars eat cloth, carpets and curtains. The very similar house moth caterpillar is just as much a pest in dried nuts, and will even eat the outsides of tennis balls.

Other household pests include flour, meal and wax moths. As their names tell us, their caterpillars eat our foods or the wax in beehives. There is even a moth called the wine moth; its caterpillar eats the cork in wine bottles.

A few types of butterflies and moths have given up plant foods. Their caterpillars prefer flesh. Most types attack aphids or other soft-bodied insects. A few types will even eat their smaller brothers and sisters.

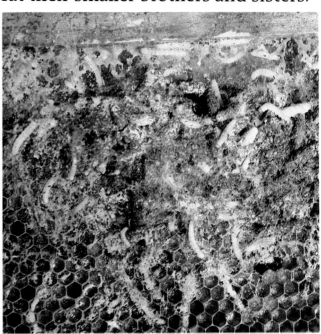

Wax moth larvae eat the wax in beehives, doing great damage.

Changing into a Pupa

When fully grown, the caterpillar stops eating and looks for a good place in which to make the change into a pupa. Most butterfly caterpillars look for a firm leaf or twig, while moth caterpillars usually burrow down into the soil or into the stem of a plant.

Butterfly caterpillars begin their change by spinning a pad of silk on a leaf or twig. They then fix their back pair of prolegs, called claspers, to the silk. Some types hang from the silk, others stay upright and spin a belt of silk around their bodies to hold them firm.

Nothing seems to happen for a few hours and then the caterpillar starts to wriggle. A tiny split appears in the caterpillar's skin behind the head. This soon opens up until the pupa begins to poke through the gap. The

A monarch butterfly pupa. Its wings can be seen through the pupal shell.

pupa wriggles until all the old skin has been pushed off. A butterfly pupa is called a chrysalis.

Moth caterpillars change into pupae in a similar way. The big difference is that they first spin a silken case, or **cocoon**, around themselves in the soil. Some moths spin cocoons attached to plants.

All pupae have hard shells on which we can see the outline of the adult's wings, tongue, legs, and abdomen. Butterfly chrysalides are sometimes decorated with gold or silver spots. Moth pupae are almost always dark brown, red, or black.

Inside the pupa a wonderful change takes place. The body of the caterpillar is broken down into liquid and from this "soup" an adult insect is slowly built up. In some butterflies and moths the pupal stage lasts only a few days; in others it may last weeks or months.

The unusual net cocoon of a moth pupa from South America.

3
The Daily Life of a Butterfly or Moth

An "89" butterfly feeding on the nectar from a flower.

Resting and Feeding

Butterflies and day-flying moths spend most of their time feeding. They flit from flower to flower, stopping only to sip the sweet nectar. As the sun sets, these flower visitors settle down for the night. They rest under tree leaves or among plants until the morning sun warms them enough for flight.

Most moths spend the day resting on tree trunks, rocks or among plants. As night falls, they crawl out from their hiding places to feed. They usually "shiver" before flying. This helps them to warm up their muscles. Their warmth is kept in by the furry hairs all over their bodies.

Most moths and butterflies cannot feed on solid food. Their tongues are only able to suck up liquids. They feed on nectar or the sweet sap that oozes from tree trunks. This kind of food gives the moths and butterflies energy for flying.

A few moths, such as silk moths, cannot feed at all. Their tongues are tiny and useless. They live on the fat stored up in their bodies when they were caterpillars. One or two types of butterflies can also get food from pollen. As they feed on the nectar in flowers, pollen sticks to their long tongues. Later they dissolve it to eat.

Many forest butterflies and moths feed on a thick, sticky substance produced by aphids. This is called honeydew. It often covers the leaves of trees and bushes. Some also feed on the juices of dead animals, on dung, or on live animals' tears.

Moths feeding on rotting fruit.

Finding a Mate

Adult butterflies and moths do not live for long. Most die after a week, although in cold countries some hibernate in winter and may live for up to nine months. During their short lives they must mate and lay eggs to continue the **life cycle**.

Only females lay eggs. However, they must first mate with a male of their own kind. This is often the first task of a female butterfly or moth after emerging from the pupa.

It is usually the male butterfly that searches for the female. All she has to do is sit with her wings open, or visit a patch of flowers and wait for a male to find her. The males of some species fly here and there, hoping to come across a female. In other types, the males stay in one small patch called a **territory**. Within this area they will chase off any other males and try to

A male and a female meadow brown butterfly mating.

mate with any females that fly nearby.

Male butterflies recognize females by their color patterns. They can do this from almost 1 m (3 ft) away. However, a male will only mate with a female if she gives the right signals. Sometimes the females hold their wings a certain way. Most females also have a special way of flicking their wings to tell a male that they have already mated.

Moths use scents to attract a mate. Most types fly at night and so cannot find a mate by sight. The female moth does all the work in attracting a male. She produces a special scent from glands at the end of her abdomen. Each kind of moth produces a different smell. Male moths use their antennae to pick up these scents.

Zebra butterflies courting. The male flies around while the female rests.

Laying Eggs

After mating, the female butterfly or moth spends her time laying eggs. Some females simply stick their eggs to a leaf, using a special glue from their bodies. Others, like the silver-washed fritillary butterfly, will carefully squeeze their eggs into cracks or holes in plant stems or bark.

Most butterflies and moths lay between 100 and 500 eggs. A few lay only 20 to 30 large eggs, while some moths can lay 5,000 or more tiny eggs. Very few eggs survive to hatch.

Each female moth or butterfly searches for the right place in which to lay eggs. Most search for a plant that can be eaten by the caterpillar. Butterflies and moths "taste" with their feet, antennae, or the tip of the abdomen. They can identify plants by sensing their colors, tastes, smells, or roughness.

A female butterfly or moth usually flutters around the plant before landing on it. After landing she may tap on the leaf with her feet or antennae. By doing this she can taste the leaf and make sure her choice was right. Once certain that she has found the right plant she will use her

A female imperial blue butterfly laying eggs on tree bark in Australia.

abdomen to find a good place to lay her eggs.

Female butterflies and moths usually lay their eggs one at a time. Those, like the marbled white butterfly, that lay large numbers of eggs, often place them in batches or simply scatter them as they fly.

A female silk moth laying eggs.

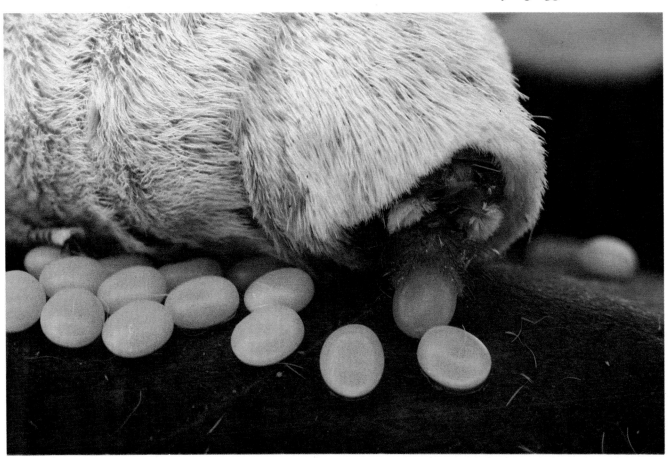

4
Colors for a Purpose

A garden tiger moth shows off its black and red warning colors.

Colors for Defense

Few butterflies and moths reach old age; most will be eaten by some other creature. The color patterns found on many butterflies and moths help them to escape their enemies.

One good way to avoid being eaten is to be poisonous to other animals. Most poisonous butterflies, moths, caterpillars or pupae are red and black or yellow and black. These colors are recognized by all creatures as a warning. In other animals they may warn of a dangerous bite or sting. In moths and butterflies they warn other creatures that they are not safe to eat.

Many very colorful caterpillars are avoided by **predators** because they contain poisons. The caterpillars get these poisons from the plants they eat. Many poisonous caterpillars also have poisonous spines or prickly hairs

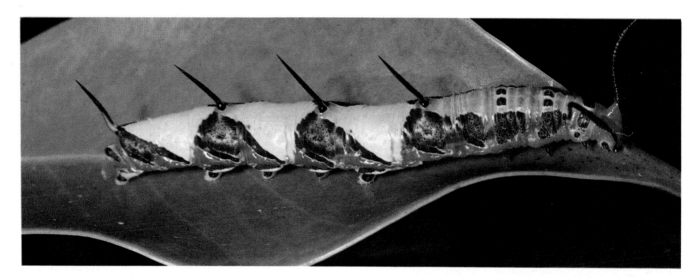

This caterpillar has the double protection of warning colors and poisonous spines.

as a double protection.

The milkweed, or monarch, butterflies are good examples of poisonous butterflies. They have poisonous caterpillars, pupae and adults. The adult butterflies have tough, leathery bodies. This helps them survive the first few pecks of birds which have not yet learned that these butterflies are poisonous.

Tiger moths and burnet moths are among the most colorful types of moths. Many are able to fly in the daytime because their warning colors show that they are poisonous, so birds and other predators keep well away from them.

Not all brightly-colored butterflies and moths are poisonous. A few types copy the patterns of the poisonous ones to fool their enemies. These copycats are called mimics.

False Eyes

The bodies of many adult butterflies and moths, as well as caterpillars, have patterns that look like eyes. Each "eye" usually has a white center and a black outer ring.

Small eyespots are common on the wings of many types of butterflies. They are usually best shown when the butterfly is feeding or resting. They act as targets for a bird's beak or a lizard's mouth. When a bird or lizard attacks a small animal it usually goes for the head end, and is attracted by the eyes. The false eyes on the other parts of the body are used to fool predators. A bird or lizard attacking the false eyes on a butterfly ends up with only a small piece of wing, while the butterfly escapes.

Large eyespots are often found on the hind wings of moths and butterflies, each wing having one

The owl butterfly from South America has a large eyespot on each wing, which makes it look like an owl.

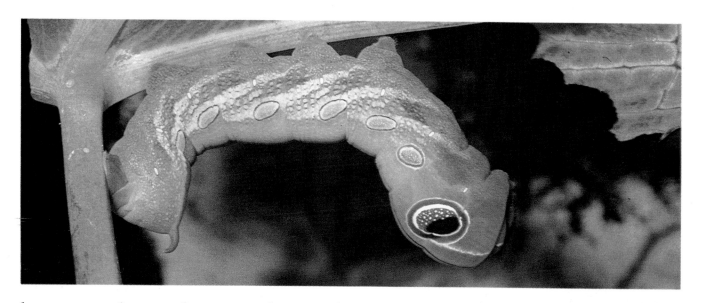

large "eye" that is often a good copy of a real eye. These "eyes" are sometimes hidden by the front wings when the moth or butterfly is at rest. If a butterfly or moth is attacked it will flash open its wings to show two huge eyes. This startles the attacker which thinks it has tackled a large animal, possibly an owl, and it is frightened away.

Some caterpillars have eyespot patterns on the front ends of their

The hawk moth caterpillar scares off its enemies by raising its head to display its large eyespots.

bodies. A few, like the elephant hawk moth caterpillars, can make these eyes seem like those of a snake; this alarms any birds attacking them. The caterpillar rears up the front of its body and pulls in its head. The two eyespots seem to grow and the caterpillar lashes around like a snake.

Camouflage

Many animals use color patterns to disguise their shapes and so avoid enemies. This is called **camouflage.** Butterflies and moths are among some of the best camouflaged animals.

Caterpillars and butterfly chrysalides are often brown or green. These colors help them to hide among leaves or on twigs. Some caterpillars are shaped and colored to look just like twigs or seed pods.

During the day, many camouflaged caterpillars keep very still and only feed at night when birds, or other predators, cannot see them.

Adult butterflies and moths often use color patterns and wing shape as part of their camouflage. Many types look like dead leaves. The angleshades moth even manages to crinkle its wings when it rests, to look like a dried-up leaf.

The best leaf-copiers are the Asian leaf butterflies. Their wings are bright blue, orange and brown on the upper side. However, the pattern on the underside of each wing is a perfect copy of a leaf, so that when they close their wings they seem to disappear. The shape and pattern includes tiny blotches and scars, just like a real leaf.

The citrus swallowtail caterpillar is not often eaten because it looks like a bird's dropping.

Hawk moths and other types of moths and butterflies, use a mixture of camouflage and warning colors to escape their enemies. Their front wings are mottled and jagged to hide them when they rest on tree trunks or rocks. If they are attacked by a predator they have an escape trick. Their hind wings are brightly colored

A moth from South America disguised as a leaf on the forest floor.

with red, blue, or orange. The moth or butterfly quickly flashes these wings at the predator just before flying away. Usually the attacker is too startled by this display to catch the moth.

Colors for Display

Moths and butterflies that find their mates by sight often have differently colored males and females. These differences may be so small that they are really only noticed by other moths and butterflies. Sometimes the males and females are so different that they look like different species.

The males of most butterflies and day-flying moths are brightly colored

Chalkhill blue butterflies courting.

so as to be noticed by other males and females. The female is usually much duller in color as she needs to avoid enemies in order to survive and lay her eggs.

The birdwing and morpho butterflies are good examples of color differences between the sexes. The males of both groups are very striking; morphos have shiny blue wings, while birdwings have bright blue, orange or green wings. The females of both groups are dark brown and usually well camouflaged in their jungle homes.

Ghost swift moths have very differently colored males and females. The females are well camouflaged with brown and orange, while the males are white on the upper sides of their wings. As night falls, the males do a strange bobbing dance over the grass where the females sit. Their white wings catch the moonlight and

may attract other males to where the females are.

Not all color differences are seen by us. Many butterflies have patterns that can only be seen in a special type of light called ultraviolet light. Unlike

The shiny blue color of the male morpho butterfly attracts females and warns off other males.

an insect's eyes, our eyes do not see this light.

5
Enemies all Around

A yellow crab spider catches a butterfly as it visits a flower.

The Enemies of Butterflies and Moths

Butterflies and moths have many enemies in all stages of the life cycle. Eggs are eaten by spiders and various insects. Caterpillars and pupae are eaten by birds, lizards, frogs, shrews, and insects such as ants and wasps. The adult moths and butterflies are eaten by birds, bats, lizards, spiders, and many other animals.

Eggs cannot move, so they make juicy meals for other insects. Eggs are protected in many ways from being eaten by predators. The tussock moth's eggs are covered with prickly, stinging hairs. The eggs of other moths and butterflies are disguised to look like tiny red blisters, or **galls**, on a leaf. A few types of eggs contain poisons that keep enemies away.

Most caterpillars depend on camouflage for defense. Others gain

Parasitic wasp eggs on a caterpillar.

protection by feeding inside plant stems or in rotting wood. A few are clothed in gaudy warning colors. The many spiny or hairy caterpillars are protected by their furry coats; most birds do not like to eat them.

Color patterns and poisons are no defense against one group of enemies. These are other insects called **parasitoids**. They include tiny wasps, called chalcid wasps, which lay their eggs in the eggs of other insects. A single moth egg can feed dozens of chalcid wasp grubs.

Caterpillars of every type of moth and butterfly are attacked by at least one type of ichneumon wasp. These wasps have long, sharp egg-laying tubes that can be stuck into the caterpillar. After hatching, the wasp grubs eat the caterpillar's insides and eventually kill it.

Ants and Butterflies

Ants are the enemies of many butterflies and moths. They eat eggs, caterpillars, pupae and adults.

Ants tend imperial blue butterfly pupae.

However, one group of butterflies has learned how to keep ants from attacking them. This group includes the blues, hairstreaks and copper butterflies. Most caterpillars and some chrysalides of this group can produce a sweet liquid from special parts of their bodies. The ants lick this liquid from the caterpillar or pupa. It is a way of bribing the ant not to attack the caterpillar.

Some blue butterflies depend on ants for protection against other insect enemies. One Australian butterfly lays its eggs on bushes near the nests of certain types of ants. Many female butterflies lay eggs on the same bush over a period of time. Caterpillars of all sizes feed there together. They are protected by the ants which drive off parasitoids and other insects. In return the caterpillars produce a sweet reward.

A few types of blue butterflies turn the tables on the ant. These types, including the large blue butterfly, feed as tiny caterpillars on flowerheads.

An ant feeds on sweet liquid made by the imperial blue caterpillar.

When large enough, they crawl down to the ground and wait for an ant of the right type to find them. The caterpillar fools the ant into thinking it is an ant larva, or grub. The ant picks up the caterpillar and carries it back to its underground nest. The caterpillar then feeds on ant grubs and eventually changes into a chrysalis in the nest. Finally, the adult butterfly crawls out of the nest, and flies away.

6
How to Study Butterflies and Moths

A red admiral butterfly on a buddleia, or butterfly, bush.

Gardens are very good places to see butterflies and moths. Their caterpillars may feed on flowers or vegetables in the garden. The adults come from miles around to feed on their favorite flowers.

In a small garden you may like to grow flowers that butterflies and moths especially like. A good one is called the butterfly bush, or buddleia. In a large garden you could leave one corner wild and perhaps even grow some wild plants that you know certain caterpillars like to eat. There are lots of books that will tell you the names of each type of butterfly and moth and what they like to eat.

A good way of learning about butterflies and moths is to watch them feeding. Notice which flowers they visit, and try and see how they push their tongues deep into each flower. Watching butterflies in the wild takes a lot of patience. You must

approach very slowly and try not to fighten them by moving quickly.

Moths are more difficult to see in the wild because most of them fly at night. A bright light will attract dozens of moths at night. A more exciting way to see them is to paint tree trunks or fence posts with a mixture of molasses and beer. Moths

A girl and her mother studying a moth.

will visit this mixture after dark to feed on the smelly, sugary liquid. You can watch them feeding if you cover the end of a flashlight with red cellophane or plastic. Moths cannot see red light; this lets you watch them without scaring them away.

Glossary

Abdomen   The rear part of an insect's body; it is made up of segments.

Antennae   The two feelers on the head of an insect. Antennae are sensitive to touch and smell.

Camouflage   The color, pattern or shape by which an animal matches its background and is therefore hidden.

Cocoon   The silky, protective case made by a moth caterpillar, and some other insect larvae, in which the pupa develops.

Compound eyes   Large eyes found on the head of an insect. Each eye is made up of many separate organs of sight and has many separate lenses.

Galls   Small blisters or growths found on plants. They usually contain the grubs of flies, wasps or mites.

Larva (plural larvae)   The grub that hatches from an insect's egg.

Lenses   The clear parts of an eye, which focus light onto the back of the eye to form a picture.

Life cycle   The series of changes, from egg to adult, in the life of an animal.

Nectar   The sugary liquid produced by flowers to attract insects.

Parasitoids   Types of insects whose larvae feed inside other insects and eventually kill them.

Predators   Animals that hunt and kill other animals for food.

Proboscis   The long tongue, or mouthpart, of certain insects, used for piercing or sucking food.

Prolegs   Short, stumpy legs found on caterpillars. They do not bend like true legs.

Pupa   An insect in the stage that comes between the larva and the adult.

Simple eyes   Eyes made of only one lens.

Territory   The area chosen by an animal in which to feed and find a mate.

Thorax   The second, or middle, part of an insect's body, bearing its legs and wings.

Veins   Tiny tubes, which carry blood inside an animal's body.

Finding Out More

The following books will help you to find out more about butterflies and moths.

Brin, Ruth. *Butterflies Are Beautiful.* Minneapolis, MN: Lerner, 1984.

Dallinger, Jane and Cynthia Overbeck. *Swallowtail Butterflies.* Minneapolis, MN: Lerner, 1982.

Jourdan, Eveline. *Butterflies and Moths Around the World.* Minneapolis, MN: Lerner, 1981

Lee, Virginia. *The Magic Moth.* Boston: Houghton Mifflin, 1972.

Massie, Diane R. *Lobster Moths.* New York: Atheneum, 1985.

Morris, Dean. *Butterflies and Moths.* Milwaukee, WI: Raintree, 1984.

Patterson, Ona. *Fragile as Butterflies.* Carthage, IL: Good Apple, 1983.

Simon, Hilda. *Milkweed Butterflies: Monarchs, Models and Mimics.* New York: Vanguard, 1968.

Index

Picture Acknowledgments

All photographs from Oxford Scientific Films by the following photographers:

G.I. Bernard *frontispiece*, 12, 18, 23, 29, 35; D. Bromhall 38; J.A.L. Cooke 8, 9, 10, 14, 15, 16, 17, 19, 22, 24, 28, 34, 39, 40, 41; S. Dalton 32; M.P.L. Fogden 31, 33; B. Frederick 13; S. Morris 25, 27; K. Porter 36; A. Ramage 20, 21; T. Shepherd 26; G. Thompson 37; P. & W. Ward 30. Artwork by Wendy Meadway.